MIRROR OF MIND

Photographs by
Russell McDougal

Foreword by José Argüelles

OPEN WINDOW BOOKS

Chickasha, Oklahoma

Open Window Books, Inc.
Box 949
Chickasha, Oklahoma 73018

Designed by Hal Hershey

Printed by Thomson-Shore, Inc.
Dexter, Michigan

I dedicate this book to all beings

*especially my family of friends and loved-ones who have
given me so infinitely much through the years.*

*and most especially my immediate family, Dan, Louann,
Nona Jane and my mother and father, so strong and so gentle,
whose tremendous love and unselfish giving have always
strengthened me and helped make this publication possible.*

We are such stuff
As dreams are made on;
And our little life
Is rounded with a sleep.

William Shakespeare

Now Suzanne takes your hand
And she leads you to the river
She is wearing rags and feathers
From Salvation Army counters
And the sun pours down like honey
On our lady of the harbour
And she shows you where to look
Among the garbage and the flowers
There are heroes in the seaweed
There are children in the morning
They are leaning out for love
And they will lean that way forever
While Suzanne holds the mirror
And you want to travel with her
And you want to travel blind
And you know you can trust her
For she's touched your perfect body
      with her mind.

Leonard Cohen

The flame started first by amazement over
subject matter, that flame which only a great
artist can have—not the emotional pleasure
of the laymen—but the intuitive understanding and recognition relating obvious reality to
the esoteric, must then be confined to a form
within which it can burn with a focused intensity: otherwise it flares, smokes and is lost
like an open bonfire.

Edward Weston, April 7, 1930, Carmel

Foreword

This unique collection of original photographs and quoteable quotes reflects a dimension of spirituality that is actually very ordinary. But the ordinariness of Russ McDougal's vision is nothing that can be defined or objectified except through direct mindfulness of everyday activity. Being the precise awareness of the flow and presence of the phenomenal world, mindfulness is spirituality experienced as nothing other than the full acceptance of this world with all of its minutiae of pain and pleasure, fullness and emptiness, shadow and light.

In attempting to convey mindfulness as an all-encompassing awareness radiating beyond a cushion in the meditation hall, Russ McDougal's work contributes to the growing possibility of an American Dharma art. This is an art of non-aggression which invites the viewer to participate in the unfolding awareness of the present, the actuality of ordinary mind. It is also the practice of seeing without bias through our own delusions as they are projected on the passing world. As we cut through our delusions the passing world may be seen clearly and precisely, neither fanciful nor frightening, but simply what is. Because of its perceptual anonymity, photography can be a particularly useful tool in this process, something of which Russ McDougal seems acutely aware.

It is my hope that the combination of words and images in this text will help convey some sense of the reality and simple beauty of the practice of mindfulness.

José A. Argüelles

Introduction

Take a look inside yourself and see that there really *is* no self, unless you create this idea conceptually. Mind is infinite, boundless, and without form. Concepts are form. You can never figure out Mind through concepts because this is trying to limit the limitless, trying to realize the formless through form. Beyond concepts and judging lies infinite freedom and the boundless space of Mind, the All Mind, The One Mind. And when you really *realize* what this means, you are free to be Free. It's been here all the time. Just awaken to It, which is You.

Mirror of Mind is not a real mirror, but a mirror, so to speak, none the less. You experience this mirror, this instant in your mind, as a focalization of all your sense impressions, including thinking. Everything takes place in consciousness and, ultimately, everything *is* consciousness. Man's whole experience is a "conscious" experience. Man and his world exist only as a reflection of each other. Take away the "world" and the "mind" disappears; take away the "mind" and the "world" disappears. The "right here" and the "right now" of this instant is the totality of your universe, as it "is". This *is* it, no more and no less. Accept it and find peace; wish it were different, and create your own suffering. It is, symbolically speaking, a reflection of your own ongoing awareness. Ongoing, like the river, always One, but never the same, yet always the same. Your Mind, constantly unfolding, like the lotus in the sun, now in this way, now in that, always One, but never the same, yet always the same. Growth, change, birth and death, yin and yang, good and bad, this and that, and on and on. Like a cosmic movie, it unfolds before you. It is you, and You are It.

To live in the Blossom of Mind, you must constantly *pay attention*. One must *stay aware* of one's consciousness. Stay awake and you will not get lost or afraid in your mind's melodramas. Find composure in the Center, while the galaxies swirl before your humbled eyes. Harmony lies amongst the chaos. There is nothing to achieve.

Clinging, condemning, and delusion create the waves in this vast ocean of Mind. Go beyond hopes and fears. One doesn't need to try to manipulate, compete with, or be bewildered by any mental projection, good or bad, presented in consciousness. Be fearless; relax. Things are simply "as they are". One has no standards to live up to. Live in that space beyond assertion and denial. Existence is a dance of patterns before the mind's eye, a living, pulsating mandala.

Ultimately, nothing exists outside Mind. Look inside and find. Look inside and see. Look inside and Be. All is a meditation.

May you see beyond these words and pictures, beyond existence and non-existence and *realize* the "One-essence", that indestructable being/non-being of everything that flows in the "Mirror of Mind".

AWAKEN!

Russell McDougal
Spring 1976

I am on a lonely road and I am traveling
  looking for the key to set me free
Oh the jealousy, the greed is the unraveling
  It's the unraveling
And it undoes all the joy that could be.

FROM "All I Want" by Joni Mitchell

The thing that hangs you up is lust, and it doesn't matter whether it's for sex or ice cream or candy bars. They're not heavy at that level.

FROM *The Caravan* by Stephen

And where do all these highways go
Now that we are free?
Why are the armies marching still
That were coming home to me?
O lady with your legs so fine
O stranger at your wheel
You are locked into your suffering
And your pleasures are the seal.

FROM "Stories of the Street" by Leonard Cohen

Learned Audience, what is sitting for meditation? In our School, to sit means to gain absolute freedom and to be mentally unperturbed in all outward circumstances, be they good or otherwise. To meditate means to realise inwardly the imperturbility of the Essence of Mind.

Learned Audience, what are Dhyana and Samadhi? Dhyana means to be free from attachment to all outer objects, and Samadhi means to attain inner peace. If we are attached to outer objects, our inner mind will be perturbed. When we are free from attachment to all outer objects, the mind will be in peace. Our Essence of Mind is intrinsically pure, and the reason why we are perturbed is because we allow ourselves to be carried away by the circumstances we are in. He who is able to keep his mind unperturbed, irrespective of circumstances, has attained Samadhi.

FROM *The Sutra of Hui Neng*

As life passes by you
On the river of time
And calls out your number
And throws you a line

Set sail for the sunrise
Fear not in the night
And if you feel yourself sinking
Reach high with your light

Find love for your neighbor
And understand his ways
'Cause love never cost you
As much as it pays

Reach high with your light
As life passes by you
On the river of time
On down to the ocean
On the river of time
To the eternal ocean
On the river of time
Reach high with your light

FROM "Reach High" by Jeffrey Cain and J. Corbitt
    (ASCAP)

seeker of truth

follow no path
all paths lead where

truth is here

BY e. e. cummings

Boy, you're gonna carry that weight, carry that weight, a long time.

FROM "Carry That Weight" by Lennon & McCartney

All paths are the same: they lead nowhere. . . . They are paths going through the bush, or into the bush. In my own life I could say I have traversed long, long paths, but I am not anywhere. My benefactor's question has meaning now. Does this path have a heart? If it does, the path is good; if it doesn't, it is of no use. Both paths lead nowhere; but one has a heart, the other doesn't. One makes for a joyful journey; as long as you follow it, you are one with it. The other will make you curse your life. One makes you strong; the other weakens you.

FROM *The Teachings of Don Juan* by Carlos Castaneda

Hark listen here he comes
Hark listen here he comes
Turning, spinning, catherine wheeling
Forever changing, there's no beginning
Speeding through a charcoal sky
Observe the truth we cannot lie

Traveling eternity road
What will you find there
Carrying your heavy load
Searching to find a peace of mind

FROM "Eternity Road" by R. Thomas (Moody Blues)

The non-action of the wise man is not
    inaction.
It is not studied. It is not shaken by
    anything.
The sage is quiet because he is not moved,
    not because he *wills* to be quiet.
Still water is like glass.
You can look in it and see the bristles on
    your chin.
It is a perfect level;
A carpenter could use it.
If water is so clear, so level,
How much more the spirit of man?
The heart of the wise man is tranquil.
It is the mirror of heaven and earth.
The glass of everything.
Emptiness, stillness, tranquillity,
    tastelessness,
Silence, non-action: this is the level of
    heaven and earth.
This is perfect Tao. Wise men find here
Their resting place.
Resting, they are empty . . .

FROM "Action and Non-Action" in *The Way of
    Chuang Tzu* by T. Merton

The clear water sparkles like crystal,
You can see through it easily, right to the
    bottom.
My mind is free from every thought,
Nothing in the myriad realms can move it.
Since it cannot be wantonly roused,
Forever and forever it will stay unchanged.
When you have learned to know in this way,
You will know there is no inside or out!

FROM *Cold Mountain* by Han Shan (Translated by
    Burton Watson)

We were talking—about the space
        between us all
And the people—who hide themselves
        behind a wall of illusion
Never glimpse the truth—then it's far
        too late—when they pass away.
We were talking—about the love we all
        could share—when we find it
To try our best to hold it there—with our
        love
With our love—we could save the world
        —if they only knew.
Try to realize it's all within yourself
        no one else can make you change
And to see you're really only very small
        and life flows on within you and without
            you.
We were talking—about the love that's
        gone so cold and the people
Who gain the world and lose their soul—
        they don't know—they can't see—are
            you one of them?
When you've seen beyond yourself—
        then you may find, peace of mind, is
            waiting there—
And the time will come when you see
        we're all one, and life flows on within
            you and without you.

FROM "Within You, Without You" by George Harrison
    (The Beatles)

That is the basic openness of compassion:
opening without demand. Simply be what
you are, be the master of the situation. If
you will just 'be,' then life flows around and
through you.

FROM *Cutting Through Spiritual Materialism* by
    Chögyam Trungpa

In all things there is nothing real,
And so we should free ourselves from the
	concepts of the reality of objects.
He who believes in the reality of objects
Is bound by this very concept, which is
	entirely illusive.
He who realizes the Essence of Mind within
	himself
Knows that the 'True Mind' is to be sought
	apart from phenomena.
If one's mind is bound by illusive
	phenomena
Where is Reality to be found, when all
	phenomena are unreal? . . .

FROM *The Sutra of Hui Neng*

"Let me take you down—'cause I'm goin' to
	Strawberry Fields.
Nothing is real, and nothing to get hung
	about.
Strawberry Fields forever.
Living is easy with eyes closed,
Misunderstanding all you see.
It's getting hard to be someone but it all
	works out,
It doesn't matter much to me."

FROM "Strawberry Fields Forever" by Lennon and
	McCartney

No matter if you're drawn to play the king or
pawn
	For the line is thinly drawn 'tween joy
		and sorrow
So my fantasy becomes reality
	And I must be what I must be and face
		tomorrow.

FROM "Flowers Never Bend With the Rainfall" by
	Paul Simon

Yes, you who must leave everything
That you can not control;
It begins with your family,
But soon it comes round to your soul.
Well, I've been where you're hanging
I think I can see how you're pinned.
When you're not feeling holy,
Your loneliness says that you've sinned.

FROM "Sisters of Mercy" by Leonard Cohen

Something you can't hide
Says you're lonely
Hidden deep inside
Of you only
It's there for you to see
Take a look and be
Burn slowly the candle of life.

FROM "Candle of Life" by J. Lodge (Moody Blues)

The process of spiritual unfoldment, to which mankind either consciously or unconsciously are parties, is a process of dissipating the *Maya*. *Maya* literally means "illusion." To a Buddha, *Maya* is the manifestation, as the *Sangsara,* of that creative energy inherent in the Cosmos, and spoken of in the *Tantras* as the Universal Mother, or *Shakti,* through whose womb embodied beings come into existence. When this energy is latent, there is no Creation and hence no *Maya*. Transcendence over *Maya,* or a going out of the realm of illusion, implies transcendence over differentiation (or separateness) and transitoriness, or, in other words, a return to primordial at-one-ment, the realization, ... of the One Mind (or Cosmic Consciousness), the re-union of the part with the whole, emancipation from the limitations of time, space, and causation, a rising out of conditioned existence into unconditioned Being *per se*, Buddhahood. The disciple must, accordingly, view the phenomenal Universe not as something to be escaped from, but as being the very essence, in symbol, of that almighty and ineffable essence of the One Mind in eternal evolution ...

FROM *The Tibetan Book of the Great Liberation* by W. Y. Evans-Wentz

The center of the Mandala is not only the external constant of space but also of time. The center of time is *now*. It is the burning tip of awareness, undefinable, for any definition in time exhausts what is *now,* and yet there is nothing but *now* and *now* is all that will ever exist. Though we can speak of past and future, the *symmetry* aspects of *now,* these only exist by virtue of the undefinable and eternal. This eternal *now* and the realization of one's center are coeval, simultaneous events. Living totally *now,* one's existence unfolds like a Mandala. At the core, each man is the center of his own compass and experiences, his own *cardinal points*—North, South, East, and West.

FROM *Mandala* by José and Miriam Argüelles

Right here and now is the ultimate as we know it. If it isn't heavy for you, then you're not tuned in, because it's very heavy here and now, and somewhere else isn't where it's heavy. This is the center of the universe, you know, and the next time . . . somewhere down the road, then that's the center of the universe, but this is too.

FROM *The Caravan* by Stephen

As long as we have some definite idea about or some hope in the future, we cannot really be serious with the moment that exists right now.

FROM *Zen Mind, Beginner's Mind* by Suzuki Roshi

So freedom lies, not in trying to become something different, nor in doing whatever you happen to feel like doing, nor in following the authority of tradition, of your parents, of your *guru,* but in understanding what you are from moment to moment.

FROM *Think On These Things* by Krishnamurti

Enlightenment is being *awake* in the nowness.

FROM *Cutting Through Spiritual Materialism* by Chögyam Trungpa

Was then not all sorrow in time, all self-torment and fear in time? Were not all difficulties and evil in the world conquered as soon as one conquered time, as soon as one dispelled time?

FROM *Siddhartha* by Hermann Hesse

. . . 'past', 'present', and 'future' are merely concepts of the limited *sangsaric* mind, . . . in the True State of the unlimited Supra-Mundane Mind there is no time, just as there is no thing. In the True State, the *yogin* realizes that even as time is, in its essentiality, beginningless and endless duration, incapable of division in past, present, and future, so space is dimensionless, and divisionless, and non-existent apart from the One Mind, or the Voidness. In other words, in the True State, Mind is the container of matter and form as of time and space.

FROM *The Tibetan Book of the Great Liberation* by W. Y. Evans-Wertz

Time is, . . . as Plotinus also teaches, . . . the measure of movement.

FROM *The Tibetan Book of the Great Liberation*

Of time you would make a stream upon whose bank you would sit and watch its flowing.
Yet the timeless in you is aware of life's timelessness,
And know that yesterday is but today's memory and tomorrow is today's dream.
And that that sings and contemplates in you is still dwelling within the bounds of that first moment which scattered the stars into space.
Who among you does not feel that his power to love is boundless?
And yet who does not feel that very love, though boundless, encompassed within the centre of his being, and moving not from love thought to love thought, nor from love deeds to love deeds?
And is not time even as love is, undivided and spaceless?

FROM *The Prophet* by Kahlil Gibran

The Perfect Way is only difficult for those
who pick and choose;
Do not like, do not dislike; all will then be
clear.
Make a hairbreadth difference, and Heaven
and Earth are set apart;
If you want the truth to stand clear before
you, never be for or against.
The struggle between 'for' and 'against' is
the mind's worst disease;
While the deep meaning is misunderstood, it
is useless to meditate on Rest.

BY Seng-ts'an in *Buddhist Texts Through The Ages,*
page 295

. . . good and evil are inseparably
one; . . . good cannot be conceived apart
from evil; . . . there is neither good *per se*
nor evil *per se.* This doctrine is expounded
in the '*Yoga* of Knowing the Mind in Its
Nakedness,' . . . Therein it is said "that the
various views concerning things are due
merely to different mental concepts. . . .
The unenlightened externally see the
externally-transitory dually. . . . As a thing is
viewed, so it appears.

FROM *The Tibetan Book of the Great Liberation* by
W. Y. Evans-Wentz

When a mind is not disturbed,
The ten thousand things offer no offence.
No offence offered, and no ten thousand
things;
No disturbance going, and no mind set up to
work; . . .

BY Seng-ts'an in *Manual of Zen Buddhism,* page 78

. . . the war between your emotions and
yourself; you and your projections, you and
the world outside, becomes transparent.
This involves removing the dualistic barriers
set up by concepts, which is the experience
of shunyata, the absence of relative concepts, emptiness.

FROM *The Myth of Freedom* by Chögyam Trungpa

Let your mind be in a state such as that of
the illimitable void, but do not attach it to
the idea of 'vacuity.' Let it function freely.
Whether you are in activity or at rest, let
your mind abide nowhere. Forget the discrimination between a sage and an ordinary
man. Ignore the distinction of subject and
object. Let the Essence of Mind and all
phenomenal objects be in a state of Thus-
ness. Then you will be in samadhi all the
time.

FROM *The Sutra of Hui Neng*

And why are you so quiet now
Standing there in the doorway?
You chose your journey long before
You came upon this highway.

FROM "Winter Lady" by Leonard Cohen

And Jesus was a sailor
When he walked upon the water
And he spent a long time watching
From his lonely wooden tower
And when he knew for certain
Only drowning men could see him
He said, "All men will be sailors then
Until the sea shall free them"
But he himself was broken
Long before the sky would open
Forsaken, almost human,
He sank beneath your wisdom like a stone.
And you want to travel with him
And you want to travel blind
And you think maybe you'll trust him
For he's touched your perfect body with his
　　mind.

FROM "Suzanne" by Leonard Cohen

Christ, as one of the most profound symbols of sacrifice, expresses the return to the center and the stripping away, the yielding of personal artifice, ambition, and ego. What is given up in the act of sacrifice is attachment to worldly attainment, including, in the case of Christ, the body itself. The cross also symbolizes the *tree of life:* only by dying to itself, by submitting to the inevitable forces of decay and disintegration and returning to the center is the tree able to grow beyond itself, even if this 'beyond' is but a mere seed once more fallen to the earth.

FROM *Mandala* by José and Miriam Argüelles

As a single person begins to see, realize and understand himself as a unique reflection and repository of the forces and energies of the whole of nature—man the conscious microcosm—so he then begins to act as an agent releasing radiant energies and attracting other beings and energies toward him. He becomes a conscious center. The attraction he exerts is not to create a system of satellites about him, but to instill this realization in others, so that all may hold together as conscious centers, each with a unique function and universal awareness and capacity for further transformation.

FROM *Mandala* by José and Miriam Argüelles

Man is the resonating agent who transforms the energies of above—of the psychic realms, and of the mind—into the energies of below—of matter, the sense-body, and the things pertaining to the senses; and vice versa. This is also the psychophysical point of view: psychic energy is continually transformed into physical energy, and physical into psychic. Man becomes the meeting ground and instrument of active and passive energies. He is the conscious center of the Mandala which heaven and earth are in the process of creating.

FROM *Mandala*

Spontaneous, expressive art automatically has a universal quality. That is why you do not have to go *beyond* anything. If you see fully and directly, then *that* speaks, *that* brings some understanding.

FROM *Cutting Through Spiritual Materialism* by Chögyam Trungpa

little sisters of the sun lit
candles in the rain
fed the world on oats and raisins
candles in the rain
lit the fire to the soul
who never knew his friend
meher baba lives again
candles in the rain
to be there is to remember
lay it down again
lay down, lay down
lay it down again
men can live as brothers
candles in the rain . . .

let your white bird smile up at the
ones who stand and frown
lay down lay down, let it all down

so raise the candles high cause if you
don't we could stay black against the night
oh raise them higher again and if you
do we could stay dry against the rain

FROM "Candles in the Rain" and "Lay Down (Candles in the Rain)" by Melanie Safka

The flame started first by amazement over
subject matter, that flame which only a
great artist can have—not the emotional
pleasure of the layman—but the intuitive
understanding and recognition relating obvious reality to the esoteric, must then be
confined to a form within which it can burn
with a focused intensity: otherwise it flares,
smokes and is lost like in an open bonfire.

Edward Weston

Each one of us must make his own true way, and when we do, that way we will express the universal way. This is the mystery. When you understand one thing through and through, you understand everything. When you try to understand everything, you will not understand anything. The best way to understand yourself, and then you will understand everything.... Before you make your own way you cannot help anyone, and no one can help you. To be independent in this true sense, we have to forget everything which we have in our mind to discover something quite new and different moment after moment.

FROM *Zen Mind, Beginner's Mind* by Suzuki Roshi

When there is no desire to satisfy yourself, there is no aggression or speed ... Because there is no rush to achieve, you can afford to relax. Because you can afford to relax, you can afford to keep company with yourself, can afford to make love with yourself, be friends with yourself.

FROM *Cutting Through Spiritual Materialism* by Chögyam Trungpa

Now you know that you are free,
Living all your life at ease.
Each day has its always,
A look down life's hallways, doorways,
To lead you there

FROM "Have You Heard? (i)" by Mike Pinder (Moody Blues)

Now you know how nice it feels,
Scatter good seed in the fields.
Life's ours for the making,
Eternity's waiting, waiting,
For you and me.

FROM "Have You Heard? (ii)" by Mike Pinder (Moody Blues)

You try being alone, without any form of distraction, and you will see how quickly you want to get away from yourself and forget what you are. That is why this enormous structure of professional amusement, of automated distraction, is so prominent a part of what we call civilization. If you observe you will see that people the world over are becoming more and more distracted, increasingly sophisticated and worldly. The multiplication of pleasures, the innumerable books that are being published, the newspaper pages filled with sporting events—surely, all these indicate that we constantly want to be amused. Because we are inwardly empty, dull, mediocre, we use our relationships and our social reforms as a means of escaping from ourselves. I wonder if you have noticed how lonely most people are? And to escape from loneliness we run to temples, churches, or mosques, we dress up and attend social functions, we watch television, listen to the radio, read, and so on. . . .

If you inquire a little into boredom you will find that the cause of it is loneliness. It is in order to escape from loneliness that we want to be together, we want to be entertained, to have distractions of every kind: *gurus,* religious ceremonies, prayers, or the latest novel. Being inwardly lonely we become mere spectators in life; and we can be the players only when we understand loneliness and go beyond it.

. . . because beyond it lies the real treasure.

FROM *Think On These Things* by Krishnamurti

Liberation (is) merely the end of error.

FROM *The Jewel Ornament of Liberation* translated by Herbert Guenther

The only way you can get in touch with your Higher Self is to not offend it, because if you offend it in any way it won't have anything to do with you. It's pure, and you've got to be as pure as it is. And where we here are timebound, your Higher Self is eternal and is in eternity, which is to say a non-space/time place . . . If you be in too much of a hurry you run out from under your Higher Self, and if you don't try hard enough you don't connect with it. But if you have real faith, and if you really move on out behind it, you can connect so that when you move, you move with the strength of the universe.

Your ego is your viewpoint, and if you lose it, you haven't got a viewpoint and you aren't in this plane anymore. That's called dying. When they say ego death it means your ego experiences what it's like to die, but you come back because it's not your time yet. The thing about ego death is your ego comes right back as soon as it's killed. It comes right back, but if you take care to keep it straight you can just watch what's going on out there and don't think about what's going on in here—don't think, "How am I doing," or "Gee, I'm neat." If you take care of business out front, then you don't get into ego trouble, but if your ego, which is your viewpoint, gets into rear-view mirrors like, "Look at me, ain't I pretty," or whatever kind of ego trip it is . . . Here's the thing about a rearview mirror: It may show you the thing in back, but it also blots out that piece of scenery that's behind the mirror. People can get so many mirrors stacked up that they ain't even seeing the scenery anymore. All they're seeing is themselves . . . if you snap to the realization that you ain't the only monkey on the planet, then you can get so you ain't so obnoxious that you make it bad for the other monkeys.

. . . you got to be cool with *this one* right now, because the trip is here and now, all the time, and if you sell out your here and now for the future you have no value in the here and now and none in the future either.

FROM *The Caravan* by Stephen

Hello dear people,
I'm writing this letter
There's something that I'd like to say
The polish is thinning, beginning to show
Through all the dulled eyes carried
    unwilling

I've stood in your streets and seen them
    change
Often I've wandered, sat here pondered
Searching the sky with my eyes

Feeling the prison is closer than before
I'd like to think it's a bad rumor
Flowers are hiding still trying to grow
Out of chaos surging around us
A new direction has to be found
The ridge pole sags to the breaking point
It is too weak for the load it must bear

Iron seems colder than before
I feel its clutches are everpresent
I'll sing a dirge for the forgotten people who
Suffered intensely because of a blindness
    and war
For the dollar and death for the scholar
The masks of the leaders are filling with
    blood
Eyes filled with silence still look out in fear
Through all the dull minds breeding
    indifference
I've lived your world and watched it dying

Farewell dear people
I'm closing this letter
With hope it will incite new growth

I've been watching the end of the cycle
    coming to pass
The end of the cycle coming to pass
I have been watching the end of the cycle
    coming to pass.

"Ku" by Barbara Mauritz and Robert Swanson

Mural: "Rainbow People"
by the *Haight-Ashbury Arts Workshop
Muralists*
(c) Miranda Bergman, Selma Brown,
Thomas Kunz, Jane Norling,
Peggy Tucker, Arch Williams

"Yes, Siddhartha," he said. "Is this what you mean? That the river is everywhere at the same time, at the source and at the mouth, at the waterfalls, at the ferry, at the current, in the ocean and in the mountains, everywhere, and that the present only exists for it, not the shadow of the past, nor the shadow of the future?"

"That is it," said Siddhartha, "and when I learned that, I reviewed my life and it was also a river, and Siddhartha the boy, Siddhartha the mature man and Siddhartha the old man, were only separated by shadows, not through reality. Siddhartha's previous lives were also not in the past, and his death and his return to Brahma are not in the future. Nothing was, nothing will be, everything has reality and presence."

FROM *Siddhartha* by Hermann Hesse

The complexities of life situations are really not as complicated as we tend to experience them. The complexities and confusions all have their one root somewhere, some unifying factor. Situations couldn't happen without a medium, without space.

FROM *The Dawn of Tantra* by Chögyam Trungpa

. . . in actual experience, variety and unity are the same. Because you create some idea of unity or variety, you are caught by the idea. And you have to continue the endless thinking, although actually there is no need to think.

FROM *Zen Mind, Beginner's Mind* by Suzuki Roshi

"The things we see," Pistorius said softly, "are the same things that are within us. There is no reality except the one contained within us. That is why so many people live such unreal lives. They take the images outside them for reality and never allow the world within to assert itself.

FROM *Demian* by Hermann Hesse

The experience of oneself relating to other things is actually a momentary discrimination, a fleeting thought. If we generate these fleeting thoughts fast enough, we can create the illusion of continuity and solidity. It is like watching a movie, the individual film frames are played so quickly that they generate the illusion of continual movement. So we build up an idea, a preconception, that self and other are solid and continuous. And once we have this idea, we manipulate our thoughts to confirm it, and are afraid of any contrary evidence. It is this fear of exposure, this denial of impermanence that imprisons us. It is only by acknowledging impermanence that there is the chance to die and the space to be reborn and the possibility of appreciating life as a creative process.

FROM *The Myth of Freedom* by Chögyam Trungpa

Because we cannot accept the truth of transiency, we suffer. So the cause of suffering is our nonacceptance of this truth. The teaching of the cause of suffering and the teaching that everything changes are thus two sides of one coin. But subjectively, transiency is the cause of our suffering. Objectively this teaching is simply the basic truth that everything changes.

FROM *Zen Mind, Beginner's Mind* by Suzuki Roshi

And the seasons they go round and round
And the painted ponies go up and down
We're captive on a carousel of time
We can't return we can only look behind
From where we came
And go round and round and round
In the circle game.

FROM "The Circle Game" by Joni Mitchell

The four *dorjes* in the gates of the inner courtyard are meant to indicate that life's energy is streaming inwards; it has detached itself from objects and now returns to the centre. When the perfect union of all energies in the four aspects of wholeness is attained, there arises a statis state subject to no more change. In Chinese alchemy this state is called the "Diamond Body," corresponding to the *corpus incorruptible* of medieval alchemy, which is identical with the *corpus glorificationis* of Christian tradition, the incorruptible body of resurrection. The mandala shows, then, the union of all opposites, and is embedded between *yang* and *yin*, heaven and earth; the state of everlasting balance and immutable duration.

FROM *The Collected Works of C. G. Jung*, vol. 9

The *center* and the *polarities:* these are the keys that unlock the language of the Mandala, as it is the Mandala that can burst the fetters of man's internal bondage and conflict by leading him to a viewpoint from which the various polarities may be harmonized. All understanding, knowledge, and principles, based as they are upon the primal duality of earth consciousness, bow before the mystery of the center, the point from which all goes forth and to which all returns. The polarities of birth and death, the attraction and repulsion of forms and forces, the past and the future are held together by the instantaneous yet eternal seed-center— the mysterious present. And these polarities: what are they but mirror-phases of the varieties of growth and transformation transmitted from the seed-centers, the points through which energy is dispersed or focalized, transformed or reborn?

FROM *Mandala* by José and Miriam Argüelles

In a minute or two the Caterpillar took the hookah out of its mouth, and yawned once or twice, and shook itself. Then it got down off the mushroom, and crawled away into the grass, merely remarking, as it went, "One side will make you grow taller, and the other side will make you grow shorter.

FROM *Alice's Adventures in Wonderland* by Lewis Carroll

. . . visualization will be inspired by a sense of hopelessness or, to say the same thing, egolessness. One can no longer deceive oneself. There is the despair of having lost one's territory; the carpet has been pulled out from under one's feet. One is suspended in nowhere or able at least to flash his non-existence, his egolessness. Only then can one visualize.

FROM *The Dawn of Tantra* by Chögyam Trungpa and Herbert Guenther

When one's vision begins to mature, one perceives the guru as the great challenger in the quest to be true to oneself.

FROM *The Dawn of Tantra*

Vision brings a new appreciation of what there is, it makes a person see things differently, rather than see different things. After all nobody can ever escape Being, least of all his own being. It is the vision that gives meaning to our experiences and our actions by making us face the problem, and therefore also vision alone gives man a sense of direction and enables him to sketch a map which will guide him in his task of finding himself rather than running away from himself.

Herbert Guenther in *Garuda IV*

The basic teaching of Buddhism is the teaching of transiency, or change. That everything changes is the basic truth for each existence . . . the teaching of selflessness. Because each existence is in constant change, there is no abiding self. In fact, the self-nature of each existence is nothing but change itself, the self-nature of all existence. There is no special, separate self-nature for each existence . . . When we realize the everlasting truth of "everything changes" and find our composure in it, we find ourselves in Nirvana.

FROM *Zen Mind, Beginner's Mind* by Suzuki Roshi

"Who are you?" said the Caterpillar.

This was not an encouraging opening for a conversation. Alice replied, rather shyly, "I-I hardly know, Sir, just at present—at least I know who I was when I got up this morning, but I think I must have been changed several times since then."

"What do you mean by that?" said the Caterpillar, sternly. "Explain yourself!"

"I can't explain *myself,* I'm afraid, Sir," said Alice, "because I'm not myself, you see."

FROM *Alice's Adventures in Wonderland* by Lewis Carroll

By ultimate fact we do not mean something eternal or something constant, we mean things as they are in each moment. You may call it 'being' or 'reality.'

FROM *Zen Mind, Beginner's Mind*

The effort to secure our happiness, to maintain ourselves in relation to something else, is the process of ego. But this effort is futile because there are continual gaps in our seemingly solid world, continual cycles of death and rebirth, constant change. The sense of continuity and solidity of self is an illusion. There is really no such thing as ego, soul or *atman.* It is a succession of confusions that create ego. The process which is ego actually consists of a flicker of confusion, a flicker of aggression, a flicker of grasping—all of which exist only in the moment. Since we cannot hold on to the present moment, we cannot hold on to me and mine and make them solid things.

FROM *The Myth of Freedom* by Chögyam Trungpa

Subhuti, it is impossible to retain past mind, impossible to hold on to present mind, and impossible to grasp future mind.

FROM *The Diamond Sutra*

To Know

Rather consists in opening out a way
Whence the imprisoned splendour may es-
cape,
Than in effecting entry for a light
Supposed to be without.

Robert Browning

conscious your tongue conscious your
dream and your thinking. . . .in this moment
when you feel what you are you get back
your self confidence . . . and you know the
responsibility is only in yourself . . . there is
not a different what you do . . . you are your
own in and outside creator . . . thinking is
energy is a reality

originally printed at the Galeria, Panajachel,
Guatemala

. . . don't ask her why she leaves to be so
free
she's gonna tell you it's the only way to be
she just can't be chained
to a life where nothing's gained
and nothing's lost
but such a cost
goodbye ruby tuesday
who is gonna hang a name on you
when you change with every new day
still I'm going to miss you
oh there's no time to lose I heard her say
you gotta catch your dreams before they run
away
dying all the time
lose your dreams and you might lose your
mind

FROM "Ruby Tuesday" by Mick Jagger and Keith
Richards

If a man gives way to all his desires, or panders to them, there will be no inner struggle in him, no 'friction', no fire. But if for the sake of attaining a definite aim, he struggles with desires that hinder him, he will then create a fire which will gradually transform his inner world into a single whole.

FROM *In Search of the Miraculous* by P. D. Ouspensky

Being infatuated by sense object, and thereby shutting themselves from their own light, all sentient beings, tormented by outer circumstances and inner vexations, act voluntarily as slaves to their own desires.

FROM *The Sutra of Hui Neng*

No appointment, no disappointment.

Swami Satchidananda

The joy of possessing does not bring us pleasure any more once we already possess something, and we are constantly trying to look for more possessions, but it turns out to be the same process all over again; so there is constant intense hunger which is based not on a sense of poverty but on the realisation that we already have everything yet we cannot enjoy it. It is the energy there, the act of exchange, that seems to be more exciting; collecting it, holding it, putting it on, or eating it. That kind of energy is a stimulus, but the grasping quality makes it very awkward. Once you hold something you want to possess it, you no longer have the enjoyment of holding it, but you do not want to let go. Again it is a kind of love-hate relationship to projections.

Chögyam Trungpa in *The Tibetan Book of the Dead,* by Francesca Fremantle and Chögyam Trungpa

In the Mind harmonious (with the Way) we
have the principle of identity,
In which we find all strivings quieted;
Doubts and irresolutions are completely
done away with,
And the right faith is straightened;
There is nothing left behind,
There is nothing retained,
All is void, lucid, and self-illuminating;
There is no exertion, no waste of energy—
This is where thinking never attains,
This is where the imagination fails to
measure.

In the higher realms of true Suchness
There is neither "self" nor "other": . . .

BY Seng-t'san in *Manual of Zen Buddhism,* page 81

Self-evaluation and self criticism are, basi-
cally, neurotic tendencies which derive from
our not having enough confidence in ourselves, 'confidence' in the sense of seeing
what we are, knowing what we are, knowing
that we can afford to open. We *can* afford to
surrender that raw and rugged neurotic
quality of self and step out of fascination,
step out of preconceived ideas.

FROM *Cutting Through Spiritual Materialism* by
Chögyam Trungpa

Now what is the Myriad Nirmanakaya?
When we subject ourselves to the least discrimination or particularization, transformation takes place; otherwise, all things remain
as void as space, as they inherently are. By
dwelling our mind on evil things, hell arises.
By dwelling our mind on good acts, paradise
appears. Dragons and snakes are the transformation of venomous hatred, while
Bodhisattvas are mercy personified. The
upper regions are Prajna crystallized, while
the underworld is only another form as-
sumed by ignorance and infatuation.
Numerous indeed are the transformations of
the Essence of Mind! People under delusion
awake not and understand not; always they
bend their minds on evil, and as a rule practice evil. But should they turn their minds
from evil to righteousness, even for a moment, Prajna would instantly arise. This is
what is called the Nirmanakaya of the
Buddha of the Essence of Mind.

FROM *The Sutra of Hui Neng*

To meet myself in beauty
To submit to the way of the Light
To realize the truth of the warrior:
    Life is suffering
Within each suffering center lies
    desire demand death
I grieve and mourn the loss of oneness
The vision of wholeness
Hidden behind the black greed of grasping
eyes
O that suffering could be seen as it is:
    A state of contraction
    And withdrawal from the Path of Light
But only by passing through the burning
flame of wisdom
Do warriors' souls become strengthened
Then do they rejoice

Dancing to the noiseless sound of the
universal
Turning one heart to all faces
Seeing one face in all hearts
Aflame with the healing power of love

The chant is blessing
The Morning Star breaks in their song
All creatures rise in radiance at its shining
And even the grasses whisper
Light is eternal
It is the eye and wellspring of the creator.

FROM *Mandala* by José and Miram Argüelles

I only know myself as a human entity; the scene, so to speak, of thoughts and affections; and am sensible of a certain doubleness by which I can stand as remote from myself as from another. However intense my experience, I am conscious of the presence and criticism of a part of me, which, as it were, is not a part of me, but a spectator, sharing no experience, but taking note of it, and that is no more I than it is you.

FROM *Walden* by H. D. Thoreau

The way of coming back is through what we might call the "abstract watcher." This watcher is just simple self-consciousness, without aim or goal . . . The abstract watcher is just the basic sense of separateness, just plain cognition of being there before any of the rest develops. Instead of condemning this self-consciousness as dualistic, we take advantage of this tendency in our psychological system as the basis of the mindfulness of effort. The experience is just a sudden flash of the watcher's being there. . . . There is just suddenly a general sense that something is happening here and now, and we are brought back. Abruptly, immediately, without a name, without the application of any kind of concept, we have a quick glimpse of changing the tone.

Chögyam Trungpa in *Garuda IV*

You are not the body, nor the body yours; you are not the doer nor the enjoyer. You are Consciousness itself, the eternal Witness, and free. Go about happily.

FROM *Astavakra Samhita* by Swami Nityaswarupananda

Breathe deep the gathering gloom,
Watch lights fade from every room.
Bedsitter people look back and lament,
Another day's useless energy spent.
Impassioned lovers wrestle as one,
Lonely man cries for love and has none.
New mother picks up and suckles her son.
Senior citizens wish they were young.
Cold hearted orb that rules the night,
Removes the colours from our sight.
Red is grey and yellow white,
But we decide which one is right
And which is an illusion???

"Late Lament" by Graham Edge (Moody Blues)

Body-consciousness is merely a monad-like, miniature reflection of the pure Consciousness with which the Sage has realized his identity. For him, therefore, body-consciousness is only a reflected ray, as it were, of the self-effulgent, infinite Consciousness which is himself.

FROM *The Spiritual Teaching of Ramana Maharshi*

Neurotic mind is a tendency to identify oneself with desires and conflicts related to a world outside. Accomplishing this projection immediately creates an uncertainty as to whether such conflicts actually exist externally or whether they are internal, whether they are really real or one is making them up. This uncertainty solidifies the whole sense that a problem of some kind exists; and this is the working basis for ego. . .

Self-Salvation (from *The Book of the Great Decease*), ii.33 (translated by T. W. Rhys David) quoted in: *The Tibetan Book of the Great Liberation* by W. Y. Evans-Wentz

Shine, Sarah, star in darkness
Warm with your amber glow
Melt into this moment
There's no where else to go.
I lie here with lovely visions,
Peaceful within the calm of now,
While yesterday, today, and tomorrow all
      bow—
And merge into a slow, swirling, pristine
      essence.
The sparkling brilliance of this silence,
The supple strength in the air—
Humbly accepting the unfolding,
What is here, we must bare.
Shine, Sarah, glow in the night
Beam as you are, beam as you might—
The infinite beckons, it is here—
Your love is so radiant, so warm, so clear.

R. McDougal ("verse to Sarah")

And when what is near you is far, then your distance is already among the stars and very large; rejoice in your growth, in which you naturally can take no one with you, and be kind to those who remain behind, and be sure and calm before them and do not torment them with your doubts and do not frighten them with your confidence or joy, which they could not understand. Seek yourself some sort of simple and loyal community with them, which need not necessarily change as you yourself become different and again different; love in them life in an unfamiliar form and be considerate of aging people, who fear that being-alone in which you trust. Avoid contributing material to the drama that is always stretched taut between parents and children; it uses up much of the children's energy and consumes the love of their elders, which is effective and warming even if it does not comprehend. Ask no advice from them and count upon no understanding; but believe in a love that is being stored up for you like an inheritance and trust that in this love there is a strength and a blessing, out beyond which you do not have to step in order to go very far!

FROM *Letters To a Young Poet* by Rainer Maria Rilke

Siddhartha listened. He was now listening intently, completely absorbed, quite empty, taking in everything . . . He could no longer distinguish the different voices—the merry voice from the weeping voice, the childish voice from the manly voice. They all belong to each other . . . They were all interwoven and interlocked, entwined in a thousand ways. And all the voices, all the goals, all the yearnings, all the sorrows, all the pleasures, all the good and evil, all of them together was the world. All of them together was the stream of events, the music of life . . . when he did not listen to the sorrow or laughter, when he did not bind his soul to any one particular voice and absorb it in his Self, but heard them all, the whole, the unity; then the great song of a thousand voices consisted of one word: Om—perfection.

FROM *Siddhartha* by Hermann Hesse

"In its true state [of unmodified, unshaped primordialness], mind is naked, immaculate; not made of anything, being of the Voidness; clear, vacuous, without duality, transparent; timeless, uncompounded, unimpeded, colourless [or devoid of characteristic]; not realizable as a separate thing, but as the unity of all things, yet not composed of them; of one taste (i.e. of the Voidness, Thatness, or Ultimate Reality), and transcendent over differentiation."

FROM *The Tibetan Book of the Great Liberation* by W. Y. Evans-Wentz

If your mind is clear, true knowledge is already yours. When you listen to our teaching with a pure, clear mind, you can accept it as if you were hearing something which you already knew. This is called emptiness, or omnipotent self, or knowing everything.

FROM *Zen Mind, Beginner's Mind* by Suzuki Roshi

Knowing Buddha means nothing else than knowing sentient beings, for the latter ignore that they are potential Buddhas, whereas a Buddha sees no difference between himself and other beings. When sentient beings realise the Essence of Mind, they are Buddhas. If a Buddha is under delusion in his Essence of Mind, he is then an ordinary being. Purity in the Essence of Mind makes ordinary beings Buddhas. With impurity in the Essence of Mind even a Buddha is an ordinary being. When your mind is crooked or depraved, you are ordinary beings with Buddha-nature latent in you. On the other hand, when you direct your mind to purity and straightforwardness even for one moment, you are a Buddha.

Within our mind there is a Buddha, and that Buddha within is the real Buddha. If Buddha is not to be sought within our mind, where shall we find the real Buddha? Doubt not that Buddha is within your mind, apart from which nothing can exist. Since all things or phenomena are the production of our mind, the Sutra says, "When mental activity begins, things come into being; when mental activity ceases, they too cease to exist."

FROM *The Sutra of Hui Neng*

So I tell you Mind is the Buddha. As soon as thought or sensation arises, you fall into dualism. Beginningless time and the present moment are the same. There is no this and no that. To understand this truth is called complete and unexcelled Enlightenment.

FROM *The Zen Teaching of Huang Po* (Translated by John Blofeld)

If he is wise he does not bid you enter the house of his wisdom, but rather leads you to the threshold of your own mind.

FROM *The Prophet* (Kahlil Gibran)

Padmasambhava is said to have described the stages of the mystic path in the following way.

1. To read a large number of books on the various religions and philosophies. To listen to many learned doctors professing different doctrines. To experiment oneself with a number of methods.

2. To choose a doctrine among the many one has studied and discard the other ones, as the eagle carries off only one sheep from the flock.

3. To remain in a lowly condition, humble in one's demeanour, not seeking to be conspicuous or important in the eyes of the world, but behind apparent insignificance, to let one's mind soar high above all worldly power and glory.

4. To be indifferent to all. Behaving like the dog or the pig that eat what chance brings them. Not making any choice among the things which one meets. Abstaining from any effort to acquire or avoid anything. Accepting with an equal indifference whatever comes: riches or poverty, praise or contempt, giving up the distinction between virtue and vice, honourable and shameful, good and evil. Being neither afflicted, nor repenting whatever one may have done and, on the other hand, never being elated nor proud on account of what one has accomplished.

5. To consider with perfect equanimity and detachment the conflicting opinions and the various manifestations of the activity of beings. To understand that such is the nature of things, the inevitable mode of action of each entity and to remain always serene. To look at the world as a man standing on the highest mountain of the country looks at the valleys and the lesser summits spread out below him.

6. It is said that the sixth stage cannot be described in words. It corresponds to the realization of the "Void" which, in Lamaist terminology, means the Inexpressible reality.

FROM *Magic and Mystery in Tibet* by Alexandra David-Neel

In the tantric tradition it is said that the discovery of the *vajra body*—that is, the innate nature of vajra (indestructible being)—within one's physical system and within one's psychological system is the ultimate experience.

FROM *The Dawn of Tantra* by Chögyam Trungpa and Herbert Guenther

We have such a strong tendency to approach our experience only as a possible confirmation of the conceptions we already have. If we are able to open, we grow. If we seek to relate everything to our preconceptions, then we are narrowing ourselves, narrowing being and we become lifeless. If we fail to see the vividness of life and try to pigeonhole it, we ourselves become pigeonholed, trapped. We must attempt to relate to this innate capacity for openness that is there, this self-existing freedom. . . . If we see things as valuable in themselves, then we will act productively so that value is retained and augmented rather than destroyed and reduced.

If we constantly relate to and defend our preconceived ideas, everything is automatically reduced to what is known as *vikalpa,* concept, which means something that is cut off from the whole. Then we have just the fragmentary world in which we are usually involved.

FROM *The Dawn of Tantra* by Chögyam Trungpa and Herbert Guenther

During countless ages, mind, in its mundane reflex, has been experiencing *sangsaric* sensuousness. Like blotting-paper incorporating ink, it has absorbed concepts. In its primordial condition it was as colourless and clear as pure water. Like drops of various coloured fluids, some almost transparent and colourless, others black as soot, so many varying concepts have been received by it that its natural transparency and colourlessness have been lost. . . . The first step in the process of removing the ink from the blotting-paper and the foreign substances from the water is dependent upon recognition of the illusory and non-real character of concepts.

FROM *The Tibetan Book of the Great Liberation* by W. Y. Evans-Wentz

The whole idea is that we must drop all reference points, all concepts of what is or what should be. Then it is possible to experience the uniqueness and vividness of phenomena directly.

FROM *The Myth of Freedom* by Chögyam Trungpa

With one hand on a hexagram
And one hand on a girl
I balance on a wishing well
That all men call the world
We are so small between the stars
So large against the sky
And lost among the subway crowds
I try to catch your eye.

FROM *Stories of the Street* by Leonard Cohen

The well is there for all. No one is forbidden
to take water from it. No matter how many
come, all find what they need, for the well is
dependable. It has a spring and never runs
dry. Therefore it is a great blessing to the
whole land. The same is true of the really
great man, whose inner wealth is inexhaustible; the more that people draw from him,
the greater his wealth becomes.

FROM *The I Ching (or Book of Changes)* (Wilhelm/
Baynes edition)

All that is harmony for thee, O Universe, is
in harmony with me as well. Nothing that
comes at the right time for thee is too early
or too late for me. Everything is fruit to me
that thy seasons bring, O nature. All things
come out of thee, have their being in thee,
and return to thee.

Marcus Aurelius

In its essence the Great Way is
     all-embracing;
It is as wrong to call it easy as to call it hard.
Partial views are irresolute and insecure,
Now at a gallop, now lagging in the rear.
Clinging to this or to that beyond measure
The heart trusts to bypaths that lead it
     astray.
Let things take their own course; know that
     the Essence
Will neither go nor stay; . . .

BY Seng-ts'an in *Buddhist Texts Through The Ages*

Were you now to practice keeping your mind motionless at all times, whether walking, standing, sitting, or lying; concentrating entirely upon the goal of no thought-creation, no duality, no reliance on others and no attachments; just allowing all things to take their course the whole day long, as though you were too ill to bother; unknown to the world; innocent of any urge to be known or unknown to others; with your minds like blocks of stone that mend no holes—then all the Dharmas would penetrate your understanding through and through. In a little while you would find yourselves firmly unattached. Thus, for the first time in your lives, you would discover your reactions to phenomena decreasing and, ultimately, you would pass beyond the Triple World; people would say that a Buddha had appeared in the world. Pure and passionless knowledge implies putting an end to the ceaseless flow of thoughts and images, for in that way you stop creating karma that leads to rebirth—whether as gods or men or as sufferers in hell.

FROM *The Zen Teaching of Huang Po* (translated by John Blofeld)

The epitome of the human realm is to be stuck in a huge traffic jam of discursive thought.

FROM *The Myth of Freedom* by Chögyam Trungpa

Thoughts link and sustain the emotions so that, as we go about our daily lives, we experience an ongoing flow of mental gossip puncutated by more colorful and intense bursts of emotion. The thoughts and emotions express our basic attitudes toward and ways of relating to the world and form an environment, a fantasy realm in which we live.

FROM *Cutting Through Spiritual Materialism* by Chögyam Trungpa

You don't do it through intellectual processes. What you do is you telepathically tap into the one great world religion, which is only one, which has no name, and all of the other religions are merely maps of *that*.

FROM *The Caravan* by Stephen

He who considers himself to be free is free indeed, and he who considers himself bound remains bound. 'As one thinks, so one becomes' is a popular saying in this world, and it is quite true.

FROM *Astavakra Samhita* by Swami Nityaswarupananda

What a man thinks of himself, that it is which determines, or rather indicates, his fate.

FROM *Walden* by H. D. Thoreau

Evermore bear in your hearts the pain and
　　sorrow of the world.
Faith thereby regaineth vigour; trim your
　　Lamps, O Tingri folk.
Life is transitory, like the morning dewdrops
　　on the grass;
Be not idle, nor give time to worthless
　　works, O Tingri folk.
Like the sunshine from a clear space twixt
　　the clouds the *Dharma* is:
Know that now there is such Sunshine; use
　　it wisely, Tingri folk.

Like the zephyr is the Free Mind,
　　unattached to any thought;
For no object have attachment; transcend
　　weakness, Tingri Folk.

Fair are the flowers in summer, then they
　　fade and die in autumn;
Likewise doth this transient body bloom and
　　pass, O Tingri folk.

Bones and flesh, though born together, in
　　the end must separate;
Think not your life a lasting good; soon it
　　endeth, Tingri folk.
Seek the True State, firm and stable, of the
　　Pure Mind, hold it fast;
That is forever the Enduring, and the
　　Changeless, Tingri folk.
Grasp the Mind, the holy treasure, best of
　　riches of man's life;
That is the only lasting treasure, O ye folk of
　　Tingri land.
Seek and enjoy the sacred elixir of
　　meditation;
Once *samadhi* hath been tasted, hunger
　　endeth, Tingri folk.
Drink ye deeply of the nectar of the Stream
　　of Consciousness. . . ."

FROM "The Last Testamentary Teachings of the Guru
　　Phadampa Sangay" in *The Tibetan Book of the*
　　Great Liberation by W. Y. Evans-Wentz

74

Therefore, O Ananda, be ye lamps unto yourselves. Be ye a refuge to yourselves. Betake yourselves to no external refuge. Hold fast to the Truth as a lamp. Hold fast to the Truth as a refuge. Look not for refuge to any one besides yourselves.

Self-Salvation (from *The Book of the Great Decease*), ii.33 (translated by T. W. Rhys David) quoted in: *The Tibetian Book of the Great Liberation* by W. Y. Evans-Wentz

Whether we see it or fail to see it, it is
    manifest always and everywhere.
The very small is as the very large when
    boundaries are forgotten;
The very large is as the very small when its
    outlines are not seen.
Being is an aspect of Non-being; Non-being
    is an aspect of Being.
In climes of thought where it is not so the
    mind does ill to dwell.
The One is none other than the All, the All
    none other than the One.

BY Seng-ts'an in *Buddhist Texts Through The Ages*

. . . From emptiness comes the
    unconditioned.
From this, the conditioned, the individual
    things.
So from the sage's emptiness, stillness
    arises:
From stillness, action. From action,
    attainment.
From their stillness comes their non-action,
    which is also action
And is, therefore, their attainment.
For stillness is joy. Joy is free from care
Fruitful in long years.
Joy does all things without concern:
For emptiness, stillness, tranquillity,
    tastelessness,
Silence, and non-action
Are the root of all things.

FROM "Action and Non-Action" in *The Way of Chuang Tzu* translated by Thomas Merton

. . . emptiness of mind is not even a state of mind, but the original essence of mind. . . . "Essence of mind," "original mind," "original face," "Buddha nature," "emptiness"—all these words mean the absolute calmness of our mind.

FROM *Zen Mind, Beginner's Mind* by Suzuki Roshi

76

So form is empty. But empty of what? Form is empty of our preconceptions, empty of our judgements . . . emptiness is also form . . .

FROM *Cutting Through Spiritual Materialism* by Chögyam Trungpa

You yourself impose limitations on your true nature of infinite Being, and then weep that you are but a finite creature. Then you take up this or that *sadhana* to transcend the nonexistent limitations. But if your *sadhana* itself assumes the existence of the limitations, how can it help you to transcend them?

Hence I say know that you are really the infinite, pure Being, the Self Absolute. You are always that Self and nothing but that Self. Therefore, you can never be really ignorant of the Self; your ignorance is merely a formal ignorance . . .

FROM *The Spiritual Teaching of Ramana Maharshi*

Your true nature is something never lost to you even in moments of delusion, nor is it gained at the moment of Enlightenment. . . . In it is neither delusion nor right understanding. It fills the Void everywhere and is intrinsically of the substance of the One Mind . . . this Void contains not the smallest hairsbreath of anything that can be viewed spacially; it depends on nothing and is attached to nothing. It is all-pervading, spotless beauty; it is the self-existent and uncreated Absolute . . . Ah, it is a jewel beyond all price!

FROM *The Zen Teaching of Huang Po* (translated by John Blofeld)

When direct identification is sought,
We can only say, 'Not two'.

In being 'not two' all is the same,
All that is is comprehended in it;
The wise in the ten quarters,
They all enter into this Absolute Reason.

This Absolute Reason is beyond quickening (time) and
    extending (space),
For it one instant is ten thousand years. . . .

FROM "On Believing in Mind" by Seng-t'san, quoted in *Manual of Zen Buddhism* by D. T. Suzuki

"What is the light of consciousness?"

It is the self-luminous existence-consciousness which reveals to the seer the world of names and forms both inside and outside. The existence of this existence-consciousness can be inferred by the objects illuminated by it. It does not become the object of consciousness.

"What is knowledge?"

It is that tranquil state of existence-consciousness which is experienced by the aspirant and which is like the waveless ocean or the motionless ether.

FROM *The Spiritual Teaching of Ramana Maharshi*

The universe rises from you like bubbles rising from the sea. Thus know the Self to be One and in this way enter into the state of dissolution.

In me, the limitless ocean, let the wave of the world rise or vanish of itself. I neither increase nor decrease thereby.

In me, the boundless ocean, is the imagination of the universe. I am quite tranquil and formless. In this alone do I abide.

In me, the boundless ocean, the ark of the universe moves hither and thither impelled by the wind of its own inherent nature. I am not impatient.

I am like the ocean and the universe is like the wave; this is Knowledge. So it has neither to be renounced nor accepted nor destroyed.

FROM *Astavakra Samhita* by Swami Nityaswarupananda

. . . a monk came to him and wanted to know how to enter unto the path of truth. Gensha asked, "Do you hear the murmuring of the stream?" "Yes, I do," said the monk. "There is a way to enter."

FROM *Zen Buddhism* by D. T. Suzuki

. . . from the statement, "Nirvana is everlasting joy," you infer that there must be somebody to play the part of the enjoyer. . . . Now it is exactly these fallacious views that make people crave for sensate existence and indulge in worldly pleasure. It is for these people, the victims of ignorance, who identify the union of five skandhas as the "self," and regard all other things as "not-self" (literally, outer sense objects); who crave for individual existence and have an aversion to death, who drift about in the whirlpool of life and death without realising the hollowness of mundane existence which is only a dream or an illusion, who commit themselves to unnecessary suffering by binding themselves to the wheel of rebirth; who mistake the state of everlasting joy of Nirvana for a mode of suffering, and who are always after sensual pleasure; it is for these people that the compassionate Buddha preached the real bliss of Nirvana.

At any one moment, Nirvana has neither the phenomenon of becoming, nor that of cessation, nor even the ceasing of operation of becoming and cessation. It is the manifestation of "perfect rest and cessation of changes," but at the time of manifestation there is not even a concept of manifestation, so it is called the "everlasting joy" which has neither enjoyer nor non-enjoyer.

FROM *The Sutra of Hui Neng*

Your stairway lies on the whispering wind.

FROM "Stairway to Heaven" by Led Zeppelin

When speech is silenced, all movement stilled, every sight and sound vanished— THEN is the Buddha's work of deliverance truly going forward! Then, where will you seek the Buddha? You cannot place a head upon your head, or lips upon your lips; rather, you should just refrain from every kind of dualistic distinction. Hills are hills. Water is water. Monks are monks. Laymen are laymen. But these mountains, these rivers, the whole world itself, together with the sun, moon and stars—not one of them exists outside your minds! The vast chiliocosms exists only within you, so where else can the various categories of phenomena possibly be found? Outside Mind, there is nothing. The green hills which everywhere meet your gaze and that void sky that you see glistening above the earth—not a hairsbreath of any of them exists outside the concepts you have formed for yourself! So it is that every single sight and sound is but the Buddha's Eye of Wisdom.

FROM *The Zen Teaching of Huang Po* (Translated by John Blofeld)

When we first experience true ordinariness, it is something very extraordinarily ordinary, so much so that we would say that mountains are not mountains any more or streams streams anymore, because we see them as so ordinary, so precise, so "as they are." This extraordinariness derives from the experience of discovery. But eventually this super-ordinariness, this precision, becomes an everyday event, something we live with all the time, truly ordinary, and we are back where we started: the mountains are mountains and streams are streams. Then we can relax.

FROM *Cutting Through Spiritual Materialism* by Chögyam Trungpa

I climb the road to Cold Mountain,
The road to Cold Mountain that never ends.
The valleys are long and strewn with stones;
The streams broad and banked with thick
    grass.
Moss is slippery, though no rain has fallen;
Pines sigh, but it isn't the wind.
Who can break from the snares of the world
And sit with me among the white clouds?

FROM *Cold Mountain* by Han-Shan

We must have beginner's mind, free from
possessing anything, a mind that knows everything is in flowing change. Nothing exists
but momentarily in its present form and
color. One thing flows into another and cannot be grasped. Before the rain stops we
hear a bird. Even under the heavy snow we
see snowdrops and some new growth.

FROM *Zen Mind, Beginner's Mind* by Suzuki Roshi

I lie alone by folded cliffs,
Where churning mists even at midday do
    not part.
Though it is dark here in the room,
My mind is clear and free of clamor.
In dreams I roam past golden portals;
My spirit returns across the stone bridge.
I have thrust aside everything that vexes
    me—
Clatter! clatter goes the dipper in the tree.

FROM *Cold Mountain*

"What is the nature of the mind?"

What is called 'mind' is a wondrous power residing in the Self. It causes all thoughts to arise. Apart from thoughts, there is no such thing as mind. Therefore, thought is the nature of the mind. Apart from thoughts, there is no independent entity called the world. In deep sleep there are no thoughts, and there is no world. In the states of waking and dream, there are thoughts, and there is a world also. Just as the spider emits the thread (of the web) out of itself and again withdraws it into itself, likewise the mind projects the world out of itself and again resolves it into itself. When the mind comes out of the Self, the world appears. Therefore, when the world appears (to be real), the Self does not appear; and when the Self appears (shines) the world does not appear. When one persistently inquires into the nature of the mind, the mind will end leaving the Self (as the residue). What is referred to as the Self is the *Atman*.

FROM *The Spiritual Teaching of Ramana Maharshi*

The subject is quieted when the object ceases,
The object ceases when the subject is quieted.

The object is an object for the subject,
The subject is a subject for the object:
Know that the relativity of the two
Rests ultimately on one Emptiness.

In one Emptiness the two are not distinguished,
And each contains in itself all the ten thousand things;
When no discrimination is made between this and that.
How can a one-sided and prejudiced view arise?

BY Seng-ts'an in *Manual of Zen Buddhism*

Most people have a double or triple notion in one activity. There is a saying, "To catch two birds with one stone." That is what people usually try to do. Because they want to catch too many birds they find it difficult to be concentrated on one activity, and they may end up not catching any birds at all! That kind of thinking always leaves its shadow on their activity. The shadow is not actually the thinking itself. Of course it is often necessary to think or prepare before we act. But right thinking does not leave any shadow. Thinking which leaves traces comes out of your relative confused mind. Relative mind is the mind which sets itself in relation to other things, thus limiting itself. It is this small mind which creates gaining ideas and leaves traces of itself.

FROM *Zen Mind, Beginner's Mind* by Suzuki Roshi

If the eyes do not close in sleep there can be
    no evil dreams;
If the mind makes no distinctions all
    Dharmas become one.
Let the One with its mystery blot out all
    memory of complications.
Let the thought of the Dharmas as All-One
    bring you to the So-in-itself.
Thus their origin is forgotten and nothing is
    left to make us pit one against the other.

BY Seng-ts'an in *Buddhist Texts Through The Ages*

Fixation could be said to be self-consciousness, which is related with dwelling on something or, in other words, perching on something. That is, you are afraid that you are not secure in your seat, therefore you have to grasp onto something, perch on something. . . . This perching process, this holding-onto-something process goes on all the time. . . . The speed comes in when you are looking constantly for something to perch on, or you feel you have to keep up with something in order to maintain your perch. Speed is the same idea as samsara, going around and around chasing one's own tail. In order to grasp, in order to perch, in order to dwell on something, you need speed to catch up with yourself. So, strangely enough, in regard to ego's game, speed and fixity seem to be complementary.

FROM *The Dawn of Tantra* by Chögyam Trungpa and Herbert Guenther

People are often hindered by environmental phenomena from perceiving Mind, and by individual events from perceiving underlying principles; so they often try to escape from environmental phenomena in order to still their minds, or to obscure events in order to retain their grasp of principles. They do not realize that this is merely to obscure phenomena with Mind, events with principles. Just let your minds become void and environmental phenomena will void themselves; let principles cease to stir and events will cease stirring of themselves. Do not employ Mind in this perverted way.

Many people are afraid to empty their minds lest they may plunge into the Void. They do not know that their own Mind IS the void. The ignorant eschew phenomena but not thought; the wise eschew thought but not phenomena.

FROM *The Zen Teaching of Huang Po* (Translated by John Blofeld)

Only when the finite mind is annihilated, is blown out like a flame of a candle by the breath of Divine Wisdom, and *Nirvana* is realized, can there be true knowing of mind. Here we have reached the frontier of the realm of terms; and progress beyond it is for the fearless, for those who are prepared to lose their life that they may find it.

FROM *The Tibetan Book of the Great Liberation* by W. Y. Evans-Wentz

To keep our mind free from defilement under all circumstances is called "Idealessness." Our mind should stand aloof from circumstances, and on no account should we allow them to influence the function of our mind. But it is a great mistake to suppress our mind from all thinking . . .

FROM *The Sutra of Hui Neng*

The mind which is always on your side is not just your mind, it is universal mind, always the same, not different from another's mind. It is Zen mind. It is big, big mind. This mind is whatever you see. Your true mind is always with whatever you see. Although you do not know your own mind, it is there—at the very moment you see something, it is there. . . . Your mind is always with the things you observe. So you see, this mind is at the same time everything.

FROM *Zen Mind, Beginner's Mind* by Suzuki-Roshi

Our original Buddha-Nature is, in highest truth, devoid of any atom of objectivity. It is void, omnipresent, silent, pure; it is glorious and mysterious peaceful joy—and that is all. Enter deeply into it by awaking to it yourself. That which is before you is it, in all its fullness, utterly complete. There is naught beside. Even if you go through all the stages of a Bodhisattva's progress toward Buddhahood, one by one; when at last, in a single flash, you attain to full realization, you will only be realizing the Buddha-Nature which has been with you all the time; and by all the foregoing stages you will have added to it nothing at all. You will come to look upon these aeons of work and achievement as no better than unreal actions performed in a dream. That is why the Tathagata said: "I truly attained nothing from complete, unexcelled Enlightenment. . . . This Dharma is absolutely without distinctions, neither high nor low, and its name is Bodhi." It is pure Mind, which is the source of everything and which, whether appearing as sentient beings or as Buddhas, as the rivers and mountains of the world which has form, as that which is formless, or as penetrating the whole universe, is absolutely without distinctions, there being no such entities as selfness and otherness.

FROM *The Zen Teachings of Huang Po* (Translated by John Blofeld)

From the reservoir of Cosmic Consciousness there now flows through the microcosmic mind of man a tiny trickle. As evolution proceeds, this trickle will grow into a rivulet, the rivulet into a deep broad river, and, at last, this river will become an infinite sea. The raindrop will have been merged into its Source.

Mind in its natural state may be compared to a calm ocean, unruffled by the least breath of air. Mind in its reflex (or *sangsaric*) aspect may be likened to the same ocean ruffled into waves by wind, the wind being the thought-process, the waves the thoughts.

FROM *The Tibetan Book of the Great Liberation* by W. Y. Evans-Wentz

Nothing save mind is conceivable. Mind, when uninhibited, conceives all that comes into existence. That which comes into existence is like the wave of an ocean. The state of mind transcendent over all dualities brings Liberation. It matters not what name may carelessly be applied to mind; truly mind is one, and apart from mind there is naught else.

Padma Sambhava from *The Tibetan Book of the Great Liberation*

To see a World in a Grain of Sand
    And a Heaven in a Wild Flower,
Hold Infinity in the palm of your hand
    And Eternity in an hour.

FROM "Auguries of Innocence" (from "Poems from
    the Pickering Manuscript") in *Blake: Complete
    Writings* (Edited by Geoffrey Keynes)

We begin to realize that there is a sane, awake quality within us. In fact this quality manifests itself only in the absence of struggle. So we discover the Third Noble Truth, the truth of the goal: that is, non-striving. We need only drop the effort to secure and solidify ourselves and the awakened state is present. But we soon realize that just "letting go" is only possible for short periods. We need some discipline to bring us to "letting be." We must walk a spiritual path. Ego must wear itself out like an old shoe, journeying from suffering to liberation.

FROM *Cutting Through Spiritual Materialism* by Chögyam Trungpa

The broken hearted people living in the
    world agree
There will be an answer, Let it be.
For though they may be parted
there is still a chance that they will see
There will be an answer,
Let it be.

FROM "Let It Be" by Lennon and McCartney

. . . So, when the shoe fits
The foot is forgotten,
When the belt fits
The belly is forgotten,
When the heart is right
'For' and 'against' are forgotten.

No drives, no compulsions,
No needs, no attractions:
Then your affairs
Are under control.
You are a free man. . . .

FROM "When the Shoe Fits" in *The Way of Chuang Tzu* translated by Thomas Merton

Voyagers of the light
    Blooming from the seed of light
    Blown into the space of eternal
        dawn. . . .
Chanting the one remembrance:
For that is the path that leads beyond
Forever, forever beyond, beyond
Knowing only that invisible force
Of which our bodies
Are the fragmentary rainbow reflection
O let us move on
Like a wind
    Blowing through the sun!

FROM *Mandala* by José and Miriam Argüelles

Sun is still shining, look at the view
Moon is still dining with me and you
Now that we're out here, open your heart
To the Universe of which we're a part

Everything's turning, turning around
See with your mind, leave your body behind
Now that we're out here open your heart
To the Universe of which we're a part

But if you want to play
stay right back on Earth
Waiting for rebirth.

FROM "Sun is still shining" by M. Pinder (Moody
    Blues)

Through the corridors of sleep past shadows
    dark and deep
My mind dances and leaps in confusion
I don't know what is real,
I can't touch what I feel
And I hide behind the shield of my illusion
So I'll continue to continue to pretend my
    life
Will never end and flowers never bend with
    the rainfall
The mirror on my wall casts an image dark
    and small
But I'm not sure at all it's my reflection
I'm blinded by the light of God and truth
    and right
And I wander in the night without direction.

FROM "Flowers Never Bend With the Rainfall" by
    Paul Simon

You have to go beyonds words and conceptualized ideas and just get into what you are, deeper and deeper. The first glimpse is not quite enough: you have to examine the details without judging, without using words and concepts. Opening to oneself fully is opening to the world.

FROM *Cutting Through Spiritual Materialism* by
    Chögyam Trungpa

The traditional Tibetian phrase defining mind—*yal la sems pena sems*—means precisely that: "That which can think of the other, the projection, is mind" . . . It contains perception, perception that is very uncomplicated, very basic, very precise. Mind develops its particular nature as that perception begins to linger on something other than oneself. That is the mental trick that constitutes mind. The tricky part is that mind makes the fact of perceiving something else stand for the existence of oneself. In fact, it should be the opposite: since the perception starts from oneself. . . .

Chögyam Trungpa in *Garuda IV*

When you do not realize that you are one with the river, or one with the universe, you have fear. Whether it is separated into drops or not, water is water. Our life and death are the same thing. When we realize this fact we have no fear of death anymore, and we have no actual difficulty in our life.

FROM *Zen Mind, Beginner's Mind* by Suzuki Roshi

Nor is it certain how long you will live. . . . Your life is like the flame of a butter lamp in a hurricane, a bubble on water, or a drop of dew on a blade of grass.

FROM *Writings of Kalu Rinpche* (Translated by Ken McLead)

It is the process of accumulation that creates habit, imitation, and for the mind that accumulates there is deterioration, death. But a mind that is not accumulating, not gathering, that is dying each day, each minute—for such a mind there is no death. It is in a state of infinite space.

So the mind must die to everything it has gathered—to all the habits, the imitated virtues, to all the things it has relied upon for its sense of security. Then it is no longer caught in the net of its own thinking. In dying to the past from moment to moment the mind is made fresh, therefore it can never deteriorate or set in motion the wave of darkness.

FROM *Think on These Things* by Krishnamurti

Life and death are one, even as the river and the sea are one.

FROM *The Prophet* by Kahlil Gibran

Bardo means gap; it is not only the interval of suspension after we die but also suspension in the living situation; death happens in the living situation as well. . . . There are all kinds of bardo experiences happening to us all the time, experiences of paranoia and uncertainty in everyday life; it is like not being sure of our ground, not knowing quite what we have asked for or what we are getting into . . . birth and death apply to everybody constantly, at this very moment.

Chögyam Trungpa in *The Tibetan Book of the Dead,* by Francesca Freemantle and Chögyam Trungpa

What is meant by a "true man"?
The true men of old were not afraid
When they stood alone in their views.
No great exploits. No plans.
If they failed, no sorrow.
No self-congratulations in success.
They scaled cliffs, never dizzy,
Plunged in water, never wet,
Walked through fire and were not burnt.
Thus their knowledge reached all the way to
    Tao.

The true men of old slept without dreams,
    woke without worries.
Their food was plain. They breathed deep.
True men breathe from their heels.
Others breathe with their gullets,
    half-strangled.
In dispute they heave up arguments like
    vomit.

Where the fountains of passion lie deep
The heavenly springs are soon dry.

The true men of old knew no lust for life,
No dread of death.
Their entrance was without gladness,
Their exist, yonder, without resistance.
Easy come, easy go.
They did not forget where from,
Nor ask where to,
Nor drive grimly forward
Fighting their way through life.
They took life as it came, gladly;
Took death as it came, without care;
And went away, yonder,
Yonder!

FROM "The True Man" in *The Way of Chuang Tzu*
    translated by Thomas Merton

We are defined not only by our place on the physical level, but by our position in consciousness, and these are an interdependent whole. *Now* is the focalization of a continuum, interrupted only by forgetfulness. The center exists continually, first as a seed, then as a stem, the trunk or the spine, and finally in the flower, where a new seed is produced. In man, consciousness—the energy and source-seed of his evolutive future—manifests through all his *nows* as so many Mandalas, so many centers around which are grouped the constituent elements of awareness. Like ripples in a pond, each awareness-moment expands out from its own center, containing in its form-pattern the configuration of all phenomena in the universe, material and immaterial. And so the process of centering—the gathering of oneself as if by an inward throw of a stone into the pool of one's own consciousness—is also a Mandala.

FROM *Mandala* by José and Miriam Argüelles

Whatever the situation, he no longer has to force results. Life flows around him. This is the basic *mandala* principle. The mandala is generally depicted as a circle which revolves around a center, which signifies that everything around you becomes part of your awareness, the whole sphere expressing the vivid reality of life.

FROM *Cutting Through Spiritual Materialism* by Chögyam C. Trungpa

The healing, meditative, integrative purpose of the Mandala has its beginning and its root in man's attempt at self-orientation. Man is the center of his own relative time/space locus from which he receives a cosmic consecration . . . and the center is always the individual, the bearer of the awareness of the eternal *now*.

FROM *Mandala*

The self loses itself and all measures, sinks into a measureless being that is without limitations, foundations, and determinations. It is devoured by being, in which no more one thing is opposed to another. In consequence, there is nothing to which the person opposes himself. This is achieved by identification with all things and events as they come along, and as they are. The self relaxes and becomes empty. The entrance of reality is no longer barred by predilections of one's own which, being peculiar to the individual, could act as a distorting medium. Things are experienced as they are, as one sees the bottom of a lake through clear and quiet water.

FROM *Contradiction and Reality* by Edward Conze (London, 1939), pp. 13–14

Go to the center and know the Whole. Follow this path. Turn inward and see with the eyes of fire the Mandala that is the Whole—I am the Mandala of the Light Eye give—this is the Path of Fire.

FROM *Mandala* by José and Miriam Argüelles

The hidden well-spring of your soul
    must
needs rise and run murmuring to the sea;
    And the treasure of your infinite depths
would be revealed to your eyes.
    But let there be no scales to weigh your
unknown treasure;
    And seek not the depths of your
      knowledge
with staff or sounding line.
    For self is a sea boundless and
      measureless.

FROM *The Prophet* by Kahlil Gibran

.. without any intentional, fancy way of adjusting yourself, to express yourself freely as you are is the most important thing to make yourself happy, and to make others happy.

. . . big mind is something to express, but it is not something to figure out. Big mind is something you have, not something to seek for.

FROM *Zen Mind, Beginner's Mind* by Suzuki Roshi

We can never be born enough. We are
    human beings;
for whom birth is a supremely welcome
    mystery,
the mystery of growing:the mystery that
    happens
only and whenever we are faithful to
    ourselves. . . .

FROM *Complete Poems 1913–1962* by e. e. cummings

There is no need to struggle to be free; the absence of struggle is in itself freedom. This egoless state is the attainment of Buddhahood.

FROM *Cutting Through Spiritual Materialism* by Chögyam Trungpa

(The Way is) perfect like unto vast space,
With nothing wanting, nothing superfluous:
It is indeed due to making choice
That its suchness is lost sight of.

Pursue not the outer entanglements,
Dwell not in the inner void;
Be serene in the oneness of things,
And (dualism) vanishes by itself.

When you strive to gain quiescence by
    stopping motion,
The quiescence thus gained is ever in
    motion;
As long as you tarry in the dualism,
How can you realize oneness?

BY Seng-ts'an in *Manual of Zen Buddhism*, page 77

Meditation is meant to be provocative. You sit and let things come up through you—tension, passion or aggression—all kinds of things come up. So Buddhist meditation is not the sort of mental gymnastic involved in getting yourself into a state of relaxation. It is quite a different attitude because there is no particular aim and object, no immediate demand to achieve something. It's more a question of being open.

FROM *The Dawn of Tantra* by Chögyam Trungpa and Herbert Guenther

. . . as you grow older you will find that your desires are never really fulfilled. In fulfillment there is always the shadow of frustration, and in your heart there is not a song but a cry. The desire to become—to become a great man, a great saint, a great this or that—has no end and therefore no fulfillment; its demand is ever for the "more," and such desire always breeds agony, misery, wars. But when one is free of all desire to become, there is a state of being whose action is totally different. It is. That which is has no time. It does not think in terms of fulfillment. Its very being is its fulfillment.

FROM *Think on These Things* by Krishnamurti

You do have to be true to yourself, but you have to be true to your best self, not to the self that wants to be heavier than other folks, or to the self that secretly thinks one is better than other people.

FROM *The Caravan* by Stephen

. . . the main point of any spiritual practice is to step out of the bureaucracy of ego. This means stepping out of ego's constant desire for a higher, more spiritual, more transcendental version of knowledge, religion, virtue, judgment, comfort, or whatever it is that the particular ego is seeking. One must step out of spiritual materialism.

FROM *Cutting Through Spiritual Materialism* by Chögyam Trungpa

O the sisters of mercy they are not
Departed or gone,
They were waiting for me when I thought
That I just can't go on,
And they brought me their comfort
And later they brought me this song.
O I hope you run into them
You who've been traveling so long.

Yes, you who must leave everything
That you can not control;
It begins with your family,
But soon it comes round to your soul.
Well, I've been where you're hanging
I think I can see how you're pinned.
When you're not feeling holy,
Your loneliness says that you've sinned.

Well they lay down beside me
I made my confession to them.
They touched both my eyes
And I touched the dew on their hem.
If your life is a leaf
That the seasons tear off and condemn
They will bind you with love
That is graceful and green as a stem.

FROM "Sisters of Mercy" by Leonard Cohen

Compassion means for you to be as adult as you are, while still maintaining a childlike quality.

FROM *Cutting Through Spiritual Materialism* by Chögyam Trungpa

And Spirit can only manifest itself on the material plane through the agency of compassionate human beings who will make themselves a reservoir for it.

FROM *The Caravan* by Stephen

Compassion becomes a bridge to the world outside. Trust and compassion for oneself bring inspiration to dance with life, to communicate with the energies of the world.

FROM *Cutting Through Spiritual Materialism*

In constantly seeking to actualize your ideal, you will have no time for composure. But if you are always prepared for accepting everything we see as something appearing from nothing . . . then at that moment you will have perfect composure.

FROM *Zen Mind, Beginner's Mind* by Suzuki Roshi

And if you can be compassionate and not revolted by anything you see so you can give people just, exact, unemotional information on the nature of their subconscious, you can help them become more sane.

FROM *The Caravan*

The great man is he who does not lose his childlike heart.

Moshi (Mencius) FROM *Zen in English Literature and Oriental Classics* by R. H. Blythe

Do not try to hold on, just observe and let go, for the most important factor is to stimulate as spontaneous a process as possible. Only from this spontaneous flow, and in this flow, does creativity arise.

FROM *Mandala* by José and Miriam Argüelles

When all the senses are stilled, when the mind is at rest, when the intellect wavers not—then, say the wise, is reached the highest state.

FROM "Katha" in the *Upanishads*

Have you ever sat very quietly without any movement? You try it, sit really still, with your back straight, and observe what your mind is doing. Don't try to control it, don't say it should not jump from one thought to another, from one interest to another, but just be aware of how your mind is jumping. Don't do anything about it, but watch it as from the banks of a river you watch the river flow by. In the flowing river there are so many things—fishes, leaves, dead animals— but it is always living, moving, and your mind is like that. It is everlastingly restless, flitting from one thing to another like a butterfly . . . just watch your mind. It is great fun. If you try it as fun, as an amusing thing, you will find that the mind begins to settle down without any effort on your part to control it. There is then no censor, no judge, no evaluator; and when the mind is thus very quiet of itself, spontaneously still, you will discover what it is to be gay. Do you know what gaiety is? It is just to laugh, to take delight in anything or nothing, to know the joy of living, smiling, looking straight into the face of another without any sense of fear.

FROM *Think on These Things* by Krishnamurti

So the whole idea is to start by relating to nonduality on a practical level, to step out of these paranoid conflicts of who in us is controlling who. We should just get into actuality, sights and sounds as they are. A basic part of the tradition of meditation is using the sense perceptions as a way of relating with the earth. They are sort of middlemen for dealing with the earth. They contain neither good nor bad, are connected with neither spirituality nor samsara, nor anything at all. They are just neutral.

Chögyam Trungpa in *Garuda IV,* page 60

The dharmata bardo is the experience of luminosity. Dharmata means the essence of things as they are, the is-ness quality. So the dharmata bardo is basic, open, neutral ground, and the perception of that ground is dharmakaya, the body of truth or law.

When the perceiver or activator begins to dissolve into basic space, then that basic space contains the dharma, contains the truth, but that truth is transmitted in terms of samsara. So the space between samsara and the truth, the space the dharma comes through, provides the basic ground for the details of the five tathagatas and the peaceful and wrathful visions.

BY Chögyam Trungpa in *The Tibetan Book of the Dead* by Chögyam Trungpa and Francesca Freemantle

So ego is the ultimate relative, the source of all the relative concepts in the whole samsaric world. . . . Even nirvana begins that way. When ego began, nirvana, the other side of the coin, began also. Without ego, there could be no such things as nirvana or liberation, since a free state without relativity would already be the case . . .

Chögyam Trungpa in *Garuda IV,* page 58–59

One in All,
All in One—
If only this is realized,
No more worry about your not being perfect!

BY Seng-ts'an in *Manual of Zen Buddhism,* page 82

Problems don't have to be solved, just let go of.

Joseph

A Mandala consists of a series of concentric forms, suggestive of a passage between different dimensions. In its essence, it pertains not only to the earth but to the macrocosm and microcosm, the largest structural processes as well as the smallest. It is the gatepost between the two.

The Mandala is earth and man, both the atom that composes the material essence of man, and the galaxy of which the earth is but an atom. Through the concept and structure of the Mandala man may be projected into the universe and the universe into man. Such mutual interpenetration is the synthesis of the various polarizing tendencies now manifest upon the planet.

The universality of the Mandala is in its one constant, *the principle of the center*. The center is the beginning of the Mandala as it is the beginning and origin of all form and of all processes, including the extensions of form into time. *In the Beginning was the Center:* the center of the mind of God, the eternal Creator, the Dream of Brahman, the galaxies that swirl beyond the lenses of our great telescopes. In all of these the center is one, and in the center lies eternity.

The center is symbolic of the eternal potential. From the same inexhaustible source all seeds grow and develop, all cells realize their function; even down to the atom there is none without its nucleus, its sun-seed about which revolve its component particles. As in the atom, so in the stars—modern thought only confirms the ancient Hermetic adage, "As above, so below." There is a structural law, a cosmic principle by which perceptible forms are sustained, and which governs the process of transformation in all things. . . .

Now is the focalization of a continuum, interrupted only by forgetfulness. The center exists continually . . . In man, consciousness—the energy and source-seed of his evolutive future—manifests through all his *nows* as so many Mandalas, so many centers around which are grouped the constituent elements of awareness. Like ripples in a pond, each awareness-moment expands out from its own center, containing in its form-pattern the configuration of all phenomena in the universe, material and immaterial. And so the process of centering—the gathering of oneself as if by an inward throw of a stone into the pool of one's own consciousness—is also a Mandala.

FROM *Mandala* by José and Miriam Argüelles

He begins to realize that the world was never outside himself, that it was his own dualistic attitude, the separation of "I" and "other," that created the problem. He begins to understand that he himself is making the walls solid, that he is imprisoning himself through his ambition. And so he begins to realize that to be free of his prison he must give up his ambition to escape and accept the walls as they are.

... The more we try to struggle, the more we will discover that walls really are solid. The more energy we put into struggle, by that much will we strengthen the walls, because the walls need our attention to solidify them.

FROM *Cutting Through Spiritual Materialism* by Chögyam Trungpa

One of the most remarkable aphorisms of oriental psychology is, "To whatever the mind goeth (or is attached), that it becometh.*

As the *Maitri Upanishad* (vi 34) teaches, "The *Sangsara* is no more than one's own thought. With effort one should therefore cleanse the thought. What one thinketh, that doth one become. This is the eternal mystery.*

FROM *The Tibetan Book of the Great Liberation* by W. Y. Evans-Wentz
*According to a private translation by E. T. Sturdy

It is the same when Siddhartha has an aim, a goal. Siddhartha does nothing; he waits, he thinks, he fasts, but he goes through the affairs of the world like the stone through the water, without doing anything, without bestirring himself; he is drawn and lets himself fall.

FROM *Siddhartha* by Hermann Hesse

Learned audience, when we use Prajna for introspection we are illumined within and without, and in a position to know our own mind. To know our mind is to obtain liberation. To obtain liberation is to attain Samadhi of Prajna, which is "thoughtlessness." What is "thoughtlessness?" "Thoughtlessness" is to see and to know all Dharmas (things) with a mind free from attachment. When in use it pervades everywhere, and yet it sticks nowhere. What we have to do is to purify our mind so that the six vijnanas (aspects of consciousness), in passing through the six gates (sense organs) will neither be defiled by nor attached to the six-sense objects. When our mind works freely without any hindrance, and is at liberty to "come" or to "go," we attain Samadhi of Prajna, or liberation. Such a state is called the function of "thoughtlessness." But to refrain from thinking of anything, so that all thoughts are suppressed, is to be Dharma-ridden, and this is an erroneous view.

FROM *The Sutra of Hui Neng*

There's a Sufi story of the river coming down to the edge of the sand and can't get across the desert, and the wind comes along and says, "Drop your identity as water and become air with me and I'll take you across the desert and turn you into water and drop you back down on the other side." And the river says, "How will I know I'll be the same river?" It doesn't matter—river is river, life is life, karma is karma. We all do our stuff. Karma's the name of the way we do it.

FROM *The Caravan* by Stephen

The Master said to me: All the Buddhas and all sentient beings are nothing but the One Mind, beside which nothing exists. This Mind, which is without beginning, is unborn and indestructible. It is not green nor yellow, and has neither form nor appearance. It does not belong to the categories of things which exist or do not exist, nor can it be thought of in terms of new or old. It is neither long nor short, big nor small, for it transcends all limits, measures, names, traces, and comparisons. It is that which you see before you—begin to reason about it and you at once fall into error. It is like the boundless void which cannot be fathomed or measured. The One Mind alone is the Buddha, and there is no distinction between the Buddha and sentient things, but that sentient beings are attached to forms and so seek externally for Buddhahood. By their very seeking they lose it, for that is using the Buddha to seek for the Buddha and using mind to grasp Mind. Even though they do their utmost for a full aeon, they will not be able to attain to it. They do not know that, if they put a stop to conceptual thought and forget their anxiety, the Buddha will appear before them, for this Mind is the Buddha and the Buddha is all living beings. It is not the less for being manifested in ordinary beings, nor is it greater for being manifested in the Buddhas.

FROM *The Zen Teaching of Huang Po* Translated by John Blofeld

. . . there are no separate realities, yours and his, for instance. There's only one reality. If you're able to deal with one end of reality, you're dealing with the whole thing.

FROM *The Dawn of Tantra* by Chögyam Trungpa

Seek within thine own self-illuminated, self-originated mind whence, firstly, all such concepts arise, secondly, where they exist, and, lastly, whither they vanish. . . . The One Mind, omniscient, vacuous, immaculate, eternally, the Unobscured Voidness, void of quality as the sky, self-originated Wisdom, shining clearly, imperishable, is Itself the Thatness.

Padma Sambhava, FROM *The Tibetan Book of the Great Liberation* by W. Y. Evans-Wentz

To see God is to BE God. There is no "all" apart from God for Him to pervade. He alone *is*.

FROM *The Spiritual Teaching of Ramana Maharshi*

In order *to do* it is necessary *to be*. And it is necessary first to understand what *to be* means.

FROM *In Search of the Miraculous* by P. D. Ouspensky

Each existence is another expression of the quality of being itself.

True being comes out of nothingness, moment after moment. Nothingness is always there, and from it everything appears . . . To have nothing in your mind is naturalness.

FROM *Zen Mind, Beginner's Mind* by Suzuki Roshi

It's there for you to see
Take a look and be
Burn slowly the candle of life.

FROM "Candle of Life" by J. Lodge (Moody Blues)

. . . They are so concerned for their life that their anxiety makes life unbearable, even when they have the things they think they want. Their very concern for enjoyment makes them unhappy . . .

I will hold to the saying that: "Perfect joy is to be without joy. Perfect praise is to be without praise."

If you ask "what ought to be done" and "what ought not to be done" on earth in order to produce happiness, I answer that these questions do not have an answer. There is no way of determining such things . . .

FROM "Perfect Joy" in *The Way of Chuang Tzu* by Thomas Merton

132

"Let it be."

J. Lennon & P. McCartney (The Beatles)

For additional copies of this book.
send $9.50 for each copy ordered (includes postage and handling) to:

OPEN WINDOW BOOKS
Box 949
Chickasha, Oklahoma 73018